WELCOME TO
PASSPORT TO READING
A beginning reader's ticket to a brand-new world!

Every book in this program is designed to build read-along and read-alone skills, level by level, through engaging and enriching stories. As the reader turns each page, he or she will become more confident with new vocabulary, sight words, and comprehension.

These PASSPORT TO READING levels will help you choose the perfect book for every reader.

READING TOGETHER
Read short words in simple sentence structures together to begin a reader's journey.

READING OUT LOUD
Encourage developing readers to sound out words in more complex stories with simple vocabulary.

READING INDEPENDENTLY
Newly independent readers gain confidence reading more complex sentences with higher word counts.

READY TO READ MORE
Readers prepare for chapter books with fewer illustrations and longer paragraphs.

This book features sight words from the educator-supported Dolch Sight Word List. Readers will become more familiar with these commonly used vocabulary words, increasing reading speed and fluency.

For more information, please visit www.passporttoreadingbooks.com, where each reader can add stamps to a personalized passport while traveling through story after story!

Enjoy the journey!

Little, Brown and Company

Hachette Book Group
237 Park Avenue, New York, NY 10017
Visit our website at www.lb-kids.com

LB kids is an imprint of Little, Brown and Company.
The LB kids name and logo are trademarks of Hachette Book Group, Inc.

The publisher is not responsible for websites (or their content)
that are not owned by the publisher.

First Edition: September 2012

ISBN 978-0-316-20993-9

10 9 8 7 6 5 4 3 2 1

IM

Printed in China

ALIENS ATTACK!

by Lisa Shea
illustrated by Dario Brizuela
coloring by Franco Riesco

LITTLE, BROWN & COMPANY
LB kids

**Attention,
all Super Hero Squad fans!
Look for these items when you read this book.
Can you spot them all?**

MAGIC WAND

ALIEN SHIP

JELLY BLASTER

LIGHTNING

It is a quiet day in Villainville,
and the villains are bored.
Nebula has an idea.
"Let us see who is the best villain."

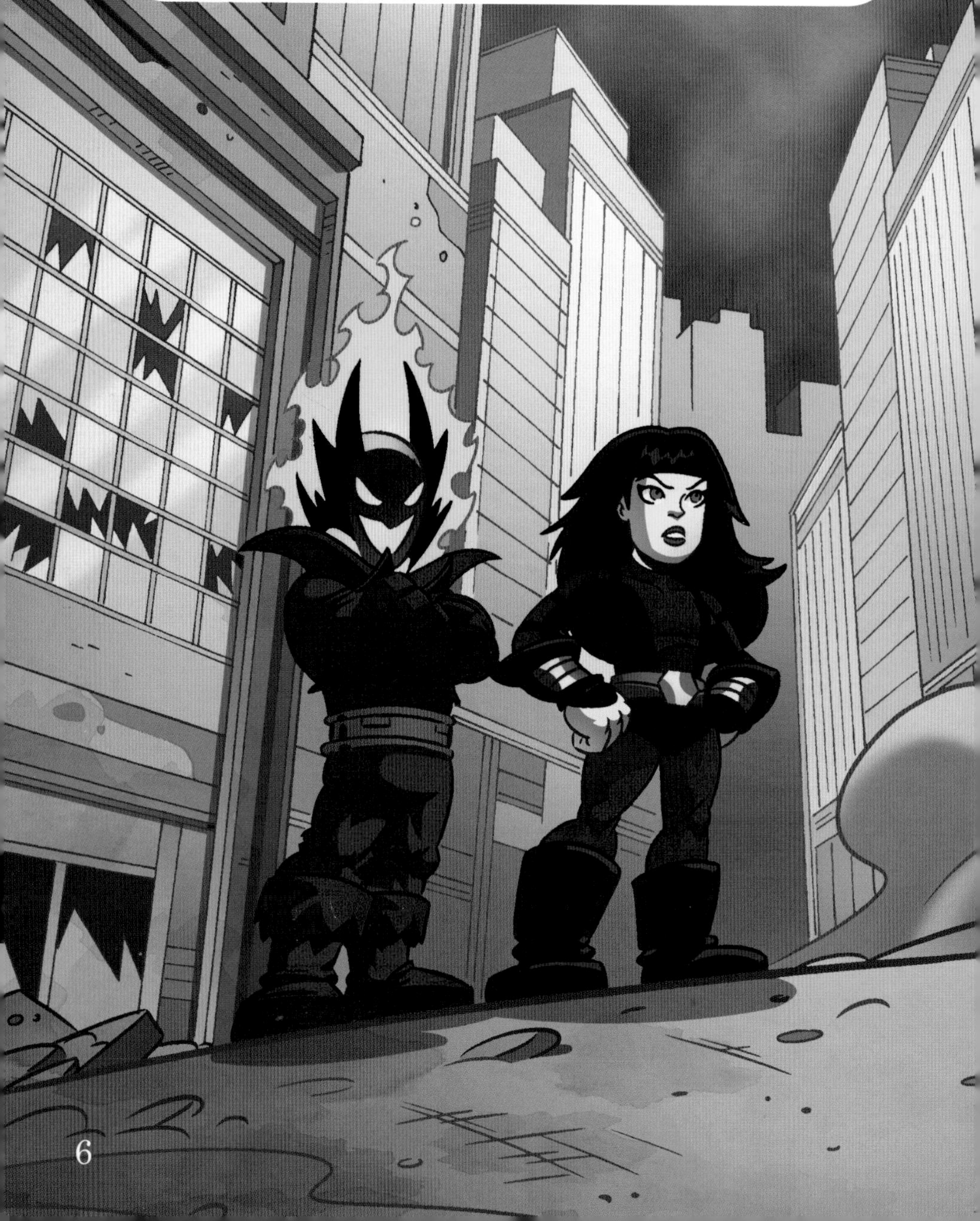

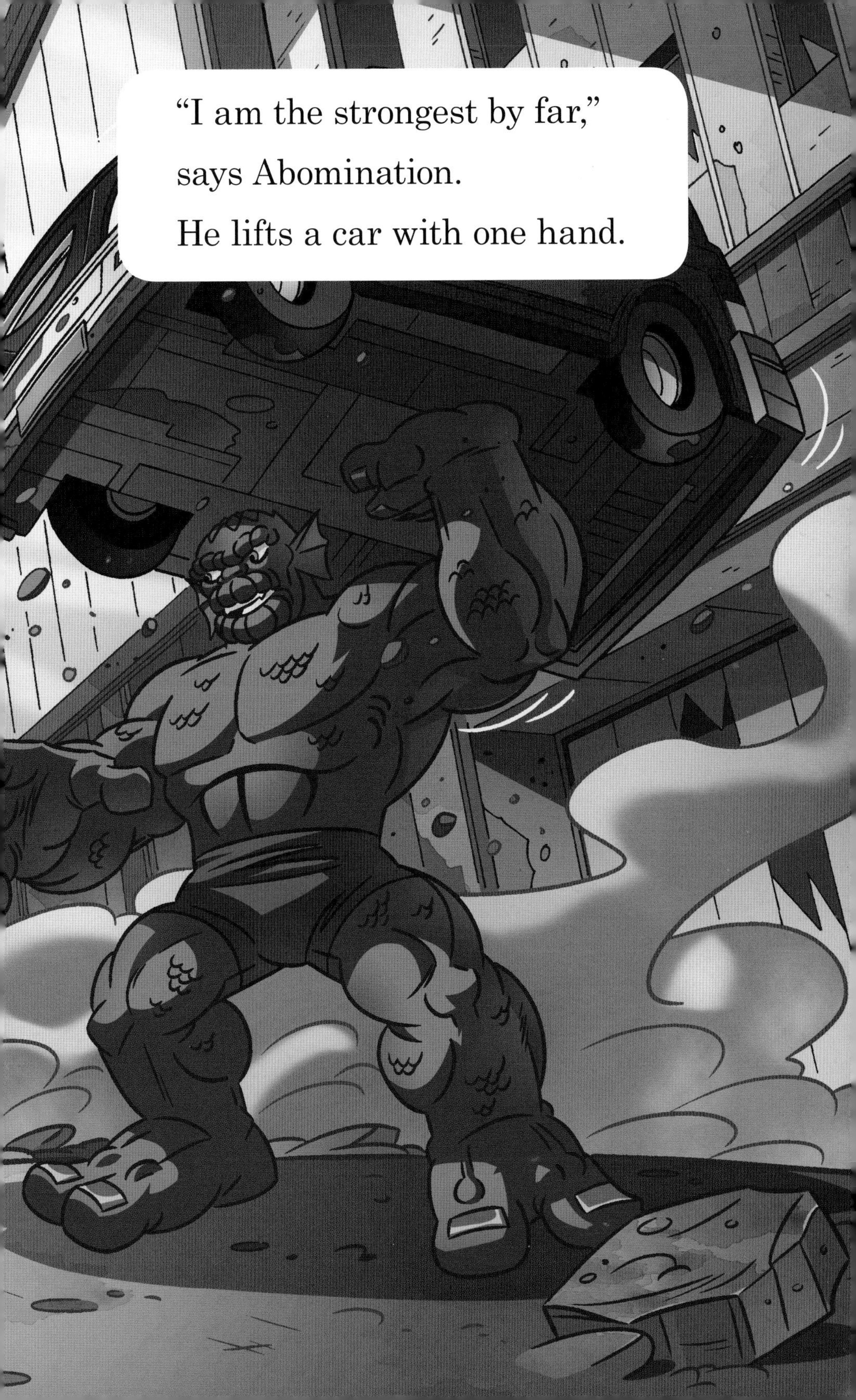

"I am the strongest by far,"
says Abomination.
He lifts a car with one hand.

"Not bad," says Dormammu.

"But watch this!"

Dormammu takes out a magic wand and aims it at the sky.

The power from the wand creates a huge black hole. "See, I am the best villain," says Dormammu.

9

Just then, Dr. Doom runs up
to the villains.
"That black hole is a doorway
between Earth and other planets,"
he cries.
"Now, aliens can come here
whenever they want."

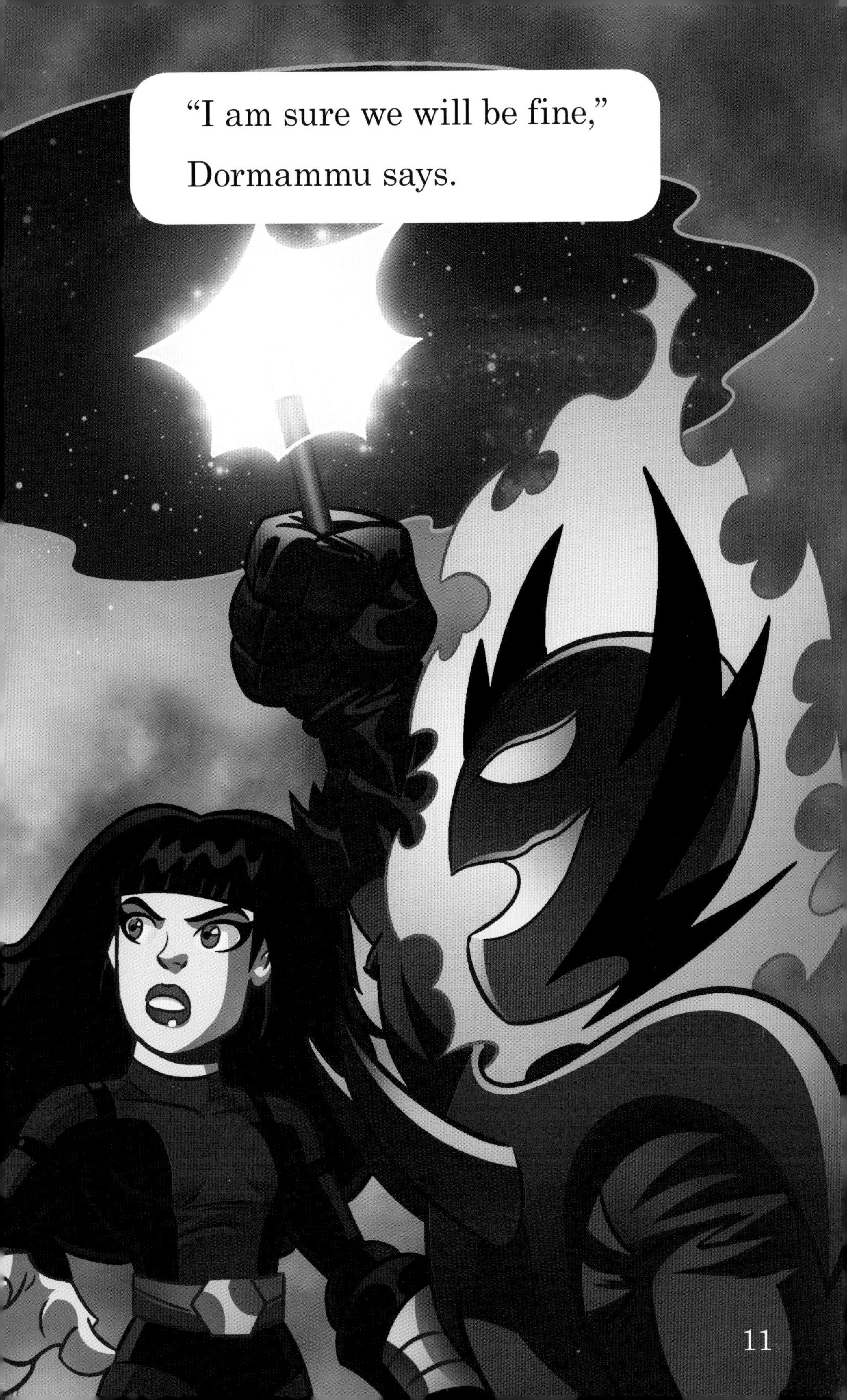

"I am sure we will be fine,"
Dormammu says.

Dr. Doom is right to worry.
That night, while everyone sleeps,
alien ships fly through the hole
and land on Earth.

The next morning,

the villains are happy to meet an alien.

"You can help us rule the world!"

Dormammu says.

"Why do we need your help?"

the alien leader asks.

"We can take over Earth without you."

At the Super Hero Squad base,
an alarm goes off.
The screen shows alien ships
over every big city.

"What should we do?"

asks Thor.

"I am from another planet, too,"

says Silver Surfer.

"I will go speak to them."

"Welcome, fellow aliens,"
Silver Surfer says to them.
"We do not want your welcome,"
the leader replies.

An alien fires at Silver Surfer
with a jelly blaster.
Silver Surfer is trapped
in a ball of pink jelly!
He cannot break free.

The aliens laugh.
"This planet is ours!"

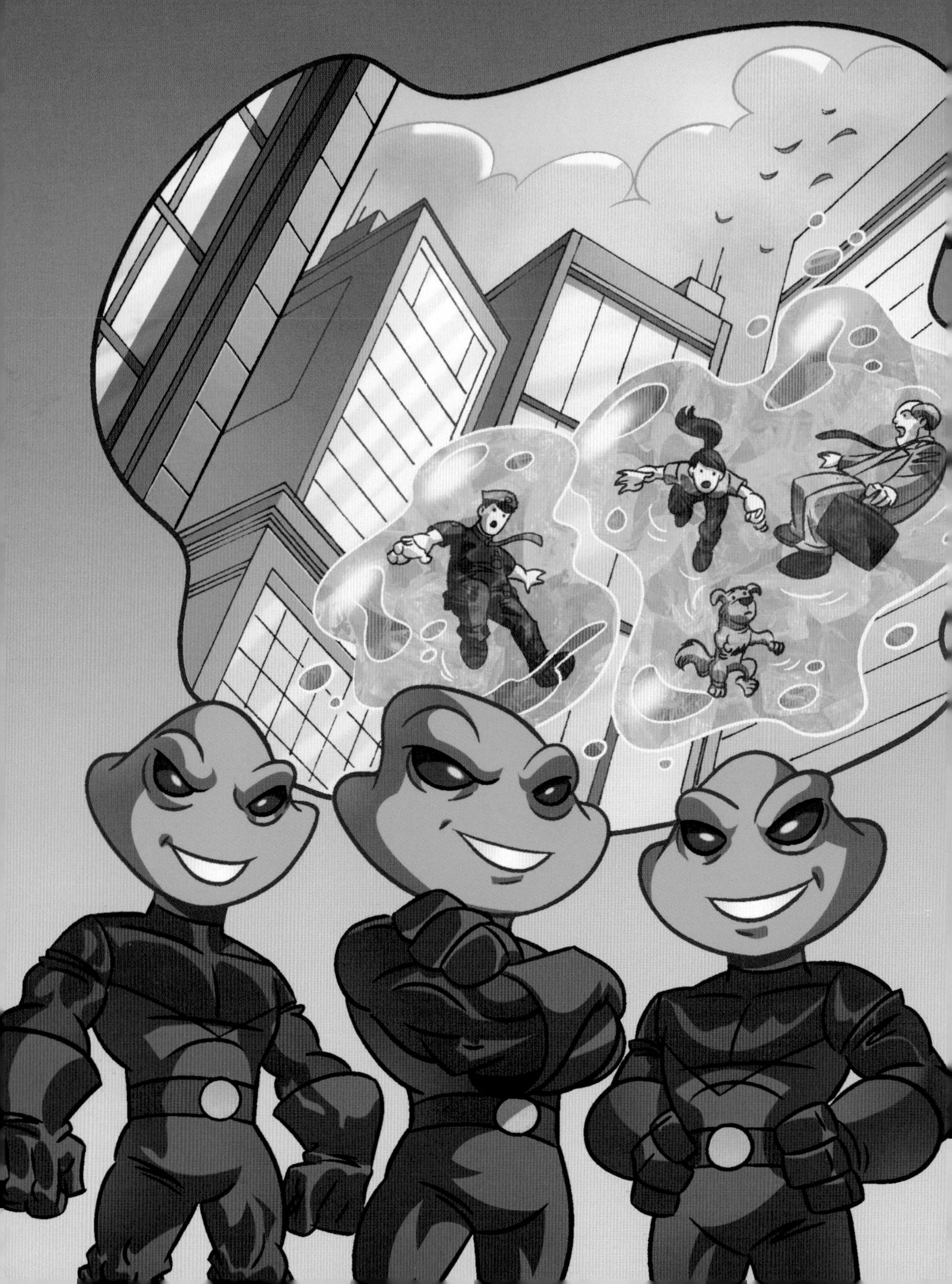

The aliens slowly catch everyone
and trap them in balls of jelly.
No one can stop them—
not even the police!

The aliens take over every city until only Super Hero City is left. The heroes will not give up without a fight!

Thor shoots lightning
from his hammer.
It bounces off the alien shields!
The aliens might win!

The villains are mad.
They want to take over
Super Hero City!
"We need to help the Squad
fight the aliens," says Dr. Doom.
"But they are our enemies!"
cries Nebula.

"We cannot take over Super Hero City
if the aliens are in charge,"
argues Dormammu.
The villains head out to find the heroes.

"We are here to help,"
Dr. Doom tells the heroes.
"I never thought I would say this,
but we are happy to see you,"
says Iron Man.

The heroes and villains
fight the aliens side by side.

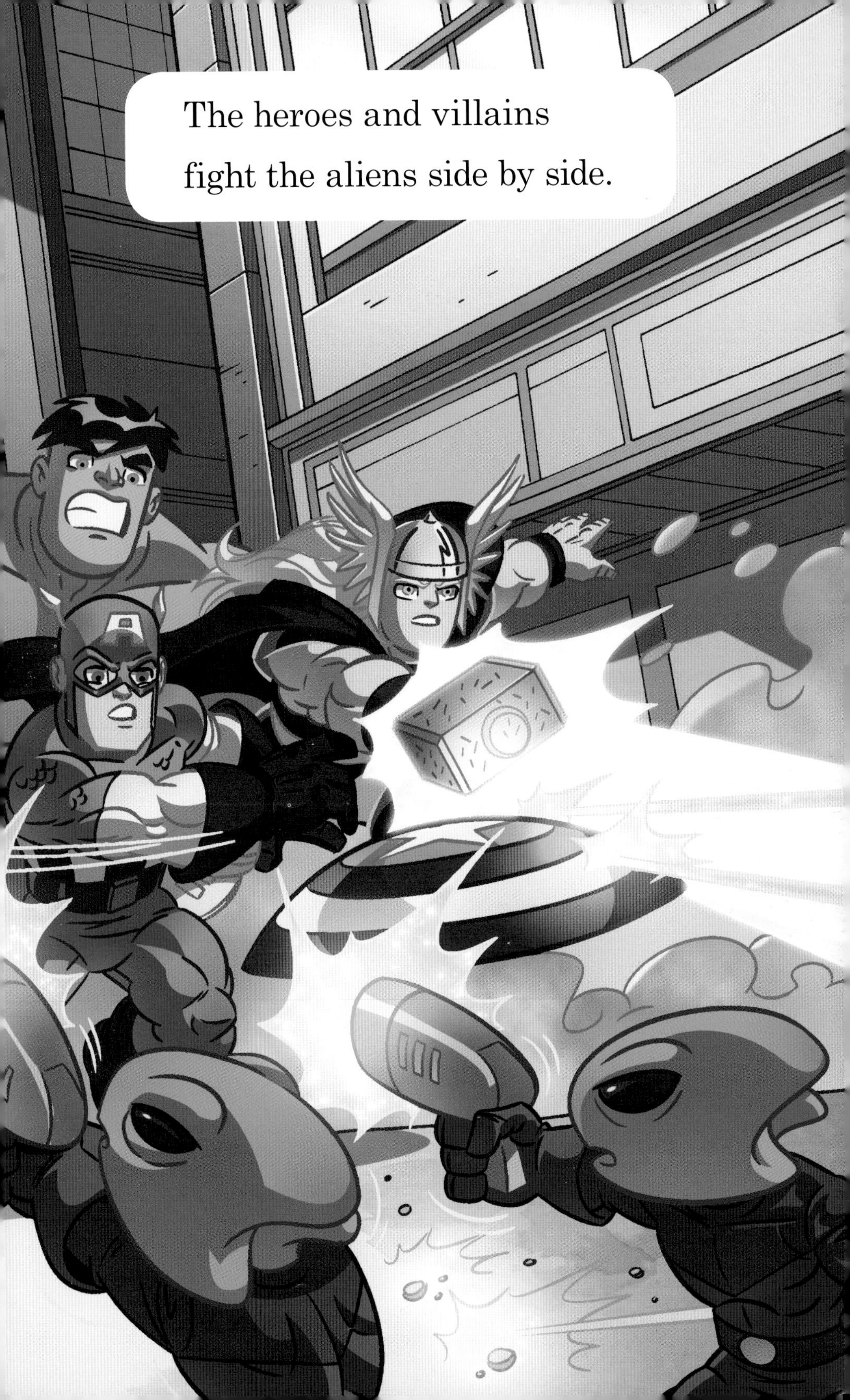

Abomination grabs a truck
and throws it at an alien ship.
Hulk picks up a bus and throws it, too.
"This is fun!" says Hulk.
Abomination smiles.

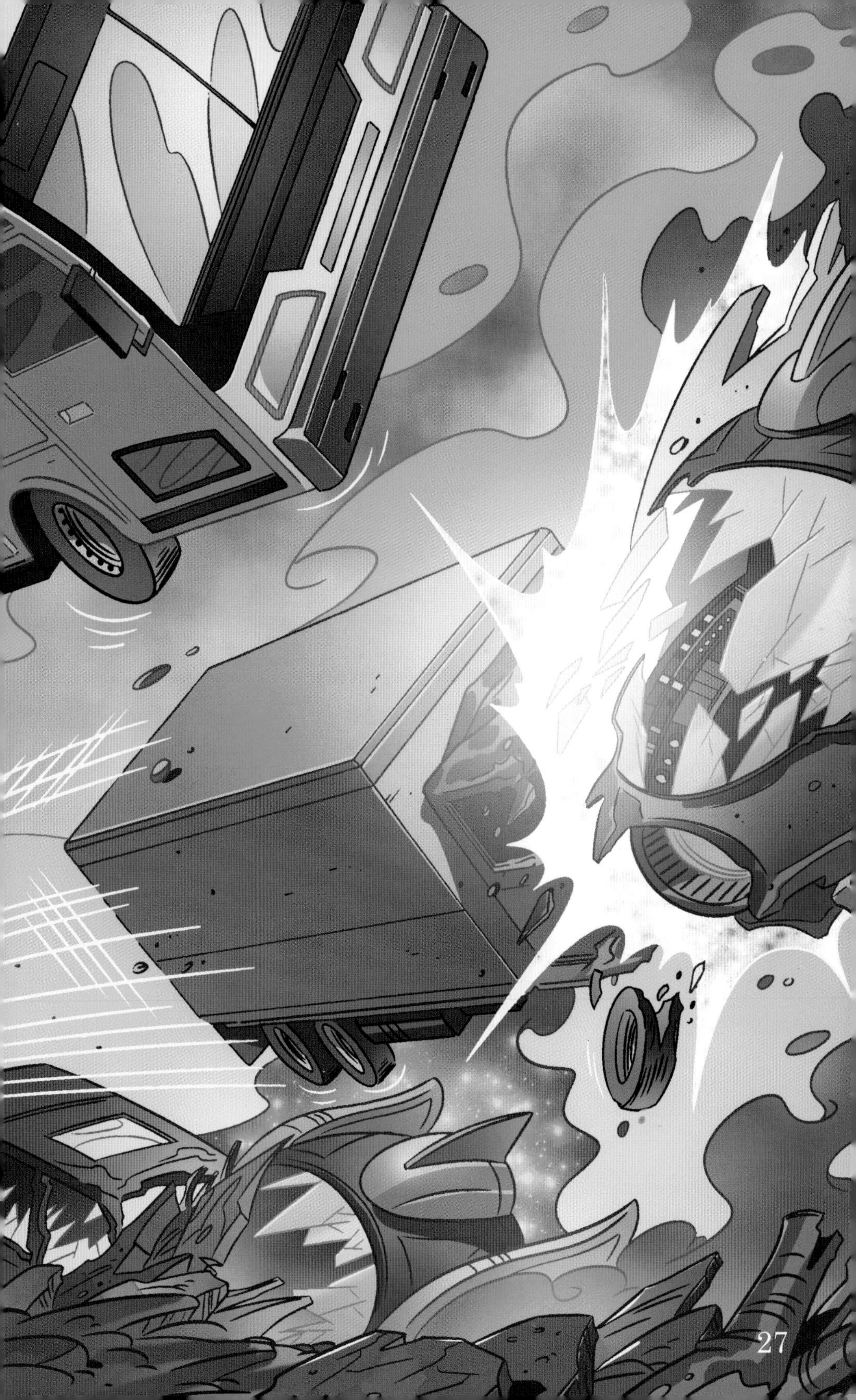

Iron Man blasts a ship
with his gloves.
"I can do better!" yells Dormammu.
He takes out the magic wand.
He zaps another ship.

The heroes and villains
surround the aliens.
"We do not like it here," the aliens say.
"We just want a quiet planet
filled with pink jelly."

The aliens get in their ships
and fly back through the black hole.
Thor shoots a thunderbolt
and seals it shut for good.
Planet Earth is safe again!

The heroes and villains free everyone
from the jelly traps.

"What a relief!" says Silver Surfer.

"I prefer peanut butter!"

"Was it so bad to work together?"
Captain America asks.

"The villains saved the day!"
Nebula yells.

"No, we did!" yell the Squaddies.

"So much for teamwork!"
Dr. Doom says with a smile.

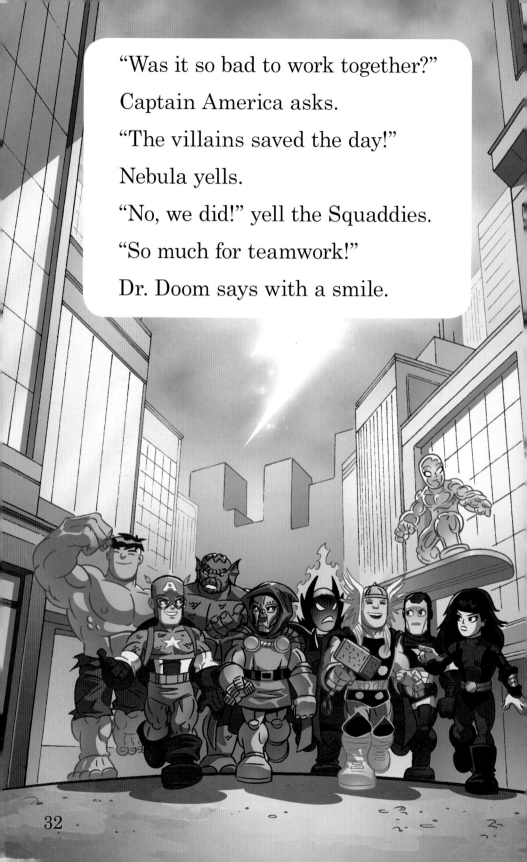